RIPLEY'S

RBI

FACT OR FICTION?

BUREAU of
INVESTIGATION

W9-AWT-100

PUBLISHING

ISBN : 978-1-893951-57-0

10 9 8 7 6 5 4 3 2 1

Design: Dynamo Limited
Text: Kay Wilkins
Interior Artwork: Ailin Chambers

For information regarding permission,
write to VP Intellectual Property, Ripley Entertainment Inc.,
Suite 188, 7576 Kingspointe Parkway, Orlando, Florida 32819

Email: publishing@ripleys.com
www.ripleysrbi.com

Manufactured in Dallas, PA, United States
in August/2010 by Offset Paperback Manufacturers

1st printing

All characters appearing in this work (pages 1-118) are fictitious and
any resemblance to real persons, living or dead, is purely coincidental.

WARNING: Some of the activities undertaken by the RBI and others in this book
should not be attempted by anyone without the necessary training and supervision.

SUB-ZERO
SURVIVAL

PUBLISHING

a Jim Pattison Company

INTRODUCING THE RBI

Hidden away on a small island off the East Coast of the United States is Ripley High —a unique school for children who possess extraordinary talents.

Located in the former home of Robert Ripley—creator of the world-famous Ripley's Believe It or Not!—the school takes students who all share a secret. Although they look like you or me, they have amazing skills: the ability to conduct electricity, superhuman strength, or control over the weather—these are just a few of the talents the Ripley High School students possess.

The very best of these talented kids have been invited to join a top secret agency—Ripley's Bureau of Investigation: the RBI. This elite group operates from a hi-tech underground base hidden deep beneath the school. From here, the talented teen agents are sent on dangerous missions around the world, investigating sightings of fantastical creatures and strange occurrences. Join them on their incredible adventures as they seek out the weird and the wonderful, and try to separate fact from fiction ...

RIPLEY

The Department of Unbelievable Lies

A mysterious rival agency determined to stop the RBI and discredit Ripley's by sabotaging the Ripley's database

The spirit of Robert Ripley lives on in RIPLEY, a supercomputer that stores the database—all Ripley's bizarre collections, and information on all the artifacts and amazing discoveries made by the RBI. Featuring a fully interactive holographic Ripley as its interface, RIPLEY gives the agents info on their missions and sends them invaluable data on their R-phones.

THE TEACHERS

▶▶ Mr. Cain

The agents' favorite teacher, Mr. Cain, runs the RBI—under the guise of a Museum Club—and coordinates all the agents' missions.

▶▶ Dr. Maxwell

The only other teacher at the school who knows about the RBI, Dr. Maxwell equips the agents for their missions with cutting-edge gadgets from his lab.

MEET THE RBI TEAM

As well as having amazing talents, each of the seven members of the RBI has expert knowledge in their own individual fields of interest. All with different skills, the team supports each other at school and while out on missions, where the three most suitable agents are chosen for each case.

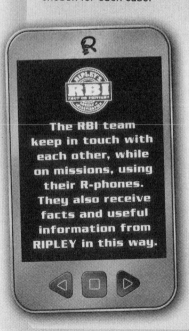

The RBI team keep in touch with each other, while on missions, using their R-phones. They also receive facts and useful information from RIPLEY in this way.

▶▶ KOBE

NAME : Kobe Shakur

AGE : 15

SKILLS : Excellent tracking and endurance skills, tribal knowledge, and telepathic abilities

NOTES : Kobe's parents grew up in different African tribes. Kobe has amazing tracking capabilities and is an expert on native cultures across the world. He can also tell the entire history of a person or object just by touching it.

▶▶ ZIA

NAME : Zia Mendoza

AGE : 13

SKILLS : Possesses magnetic and electrical powers. Can predict the weather

NOTES : The only survivor of a tropical storm that destroyed her village when she was a baby. Zia doesn't yet fully understand her abilities but she can predict, and sometimes control, the weather. Her presence can also affect electrical equipment.

▶▶ MAX

NAME : Max Johnson

AGE : 14

SKILLS : Computer genius and inventor

NOTES : Max, from Las Vegas, loves computer games and anything electrical. He spends most of his spare time inventing robots. Max hates school but he loves spending time helping Dr. Maxwell come up with new gadgets.

▶▶KATE

NAME : Kate Jones

AGE : 14

SKILLS : Computer-like memory, extremely clever, and ability to master languages in minutes

NOTES : Raised at Oxford University in England by her history professor and part-time archaeologist uncle. Kate memorized every book in the University library after reading them only once!

▶▶ALEK

NAME : Alek Filipov

AGE : 15

SKILL : Contortionist with amazing physical strength

NOTES : Alek is a member of the Russian under-16 Olympic gymnastics team and loves sports and competitions. He is much bigger than the other agents, and although he seems quiet and serious much of the time, he has a wicked sense of humor.

▶▶ LI

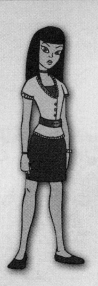

NAME : Li Yong

AGE : 15

SKILL : Musical genius with pitch-perfect hearing and the ability to mimic any sound

NOTES : Li grew up in a wealthy family in Beijing, China, and joined Ripley High later than the other RBI agents. She has a highly developed sense of hearing and can imitate any sound she hears.

▶▶ JACK

NAME : Jack Stevens

AGE : 14

SKILLS : Can "talk" to animals and has expert survival skills

NOTES : Jack grew up on an animal park in the Australian outback. He has always shared a strong bond with animals and can communicate with any creature— and loves to eat weird food!

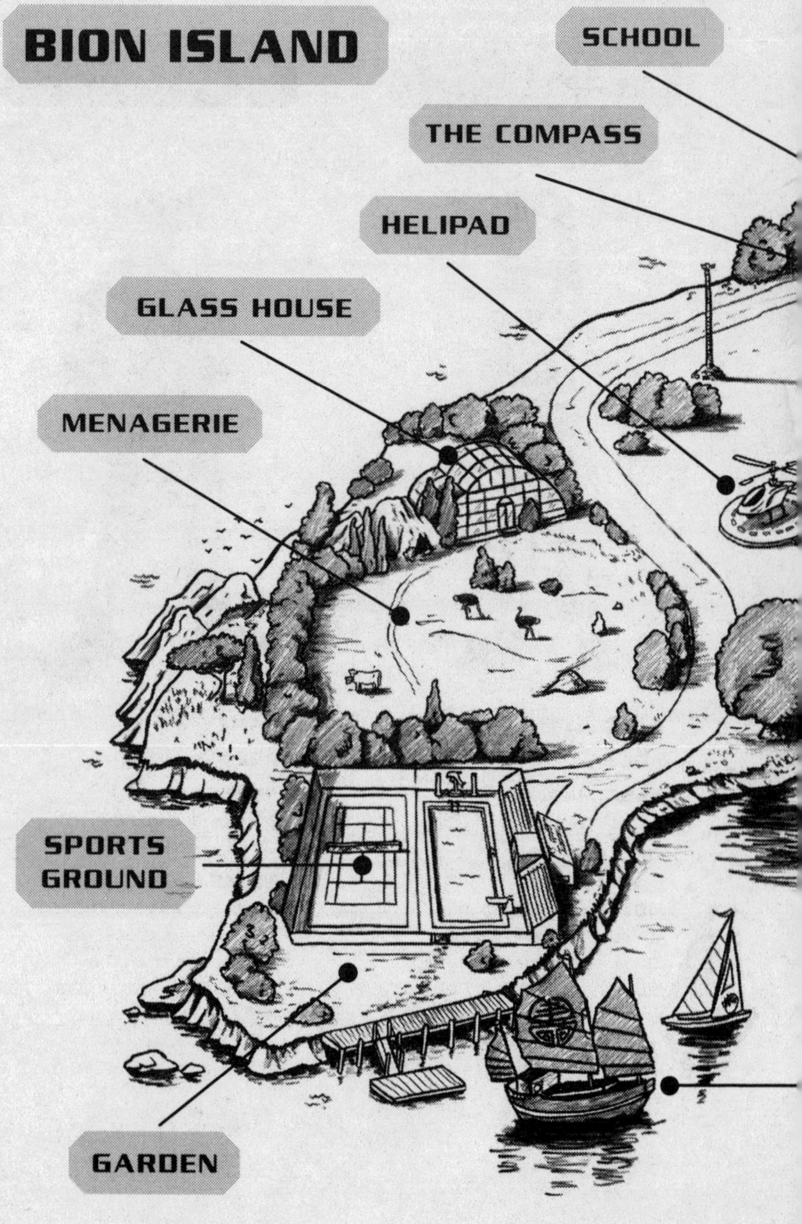

BION ISLAND

SCHOOL

THE COMPASS

HELIPAD

GLASS HOUSE

MENAGERIE

SPORTS GROUND

GARDEN

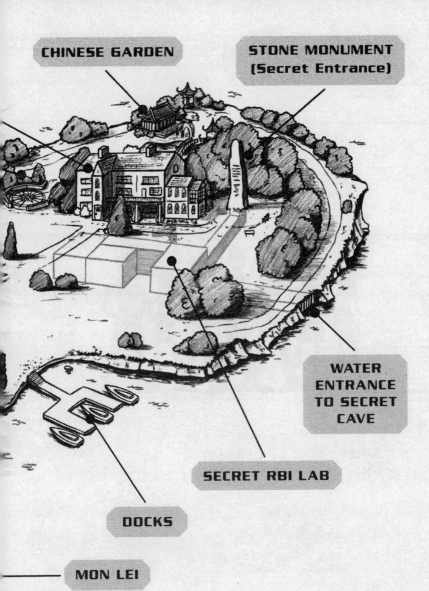

CHINESE GARDEN

STONE MONUMENT (Secret Entrance)

WATER ENTRANCE TO SECRET CAVE

SECRET RBI LAB

DOCKS

MON LEI

Prologue

A cold wind blew fiercely across the frosty wilderness, where white mounds of snow covered everything in sight. Stars shone brightly in the black sky. With no human civilization for miles, there was no man-made light to pollute the brilliance of this night scene. A chilling gale moving in from the water whipped up the surface of this truly hostile land. A group of seals sensed the change in the wind and barked to each other, giving and receiving orders. Although this place was far too harsh for man, the seals thrived in the bitter, glacial conditions. One by one, the creatures moved toward the edge of the ice floe they were on and dropped into the biting cold water below.

A dark shape cut silently through the water heading for the seals: a killer whale, hungry for a meal. It targeted a small cluster of seals on

the edge of the group as its best option and set off through the icy sea toward them.

At the last moment, the whale changed its course. Some other creature had blocked its path, a pale body rising between the whale and its prey. The seals, sensing danger, began to bark again and scurried away. The confused whale backed off for now, realizing that this disruption had taken away the advantage of surprise and allowed its meal to escape.

As the whale disappeared back into the icy waters, the pale creature joined the group of seals again. The seals swam happily beside this newcomer, a creature quite uncommon in this land of ice, and almost unbelievable in the glacial water.

The Wrong Note

"If you follow the text on page 352, it will tell you all about Robert Ripley's encounter with the Jivaros in Ecuador," Mr. Willis's voice echoed around the classroom.

"The Jivaros are the tribe who shrink human heads," Kobe told Max.

"Shrunken heads are absolutely awesome," said Max. "I can't believe that Mr. Willis can make even head-shrinking seem boring!"

"Read in silence, please, unless you want to read it in detention!" Mr. Willis shouted, his steely eyes homing in on Kobe and Max.

At the far end of the table, Kate flinched at the telling off. It was not because some of her fellow RBI agents were in trouble; Kate was used to Max being told off in every lesson. It was because she herself was dying to say something to Li who was sitting next to her.

Li had recently returned from a mission to London with a gift for Kate: a history book. Along with all the knowledge about the explorer who had written the book, Kate had discovered something much more important.

On a recent mission, the agents had found an artifact hidden years ago by Robert Ripley himself. When they brought it back to Ripley High, it had uncovered a quest that Rip had set. There were more amazing artifacts hidden around the world, and Rip had left clues on how to find them. The agents had found five clues so far and no one could work out in which direction they were pointing the team, or any links between them. Until now. The book was one of those clues and Kate thought she had found a connection between something she had read in the book and one of the other clues. She had been so keen to finish the book that she had almost been late for class for the first time in her life. She had arrived just in time, but it had left her with no chance to tell Li about her discovery, and she was almost bursting with excitement.

Kate loved all her lessons, including Mr. Willis's, which everyone else thought were the most boring things in the world, but today the clock seemed to be ticking much more slowly than normal. There was still another half hour to go! Kate couldn't stand it any longer. Quickly, she ripped a page out of her notebook and scribbled a note on it:

I've found a link between the book and one of Rip's other clues.

After folding it in half, Kate passed it to Li.

Li's eyes flashed with interest.

"What do you mean?" she whispered to her friend. "What link?"

"I said quiet!" Mr. Willis boomed, and both girls bent their heads back down over their books.

Out of the corner of her eye, though, Kate saw Alek reading a note that looked suspiciously like the one written by her. She then saw Alek pass the note to Kobe, Kobe pass it on to Zia, Zia pass it to Jack, and Jack hand the paper to Max.

"No way!" said Max, with more of a shout than a whisper.

Kate cringed, immediately knowing that she should have never passed a note on, particularly one that contained secret RBI information. She saw a similar reaction from all the RBI agents as Mr. Willis made his way over to Max.

"What is that?" he asked, pointing to the folded piece of paper in Max's hand.

"My hand, sir," Max replied.

"Give me that paper, now," the teacher instructed.

Several thoughts went through Kate's head, all of them ending with her being expelled

from Ripley High and the end of the RBI. She couldn't possibly allow that to happen; she had to think of something to stop Mr. Willis examining that note too closely and wondering what it meant.

Kate leaped up from her chair, which screeched loudly as it slid across the floor.

"It's for a story I'm working on with Max in Mr. Cain's class, and it's completely and entirely made up," she blurted out.

Mr. Willis's face was a mixture of shock and anger as he read the note. Kate wished that the floor would open up and swallow her.

"Well, Miss Jones, I am disappointed," said Mr. Willis. "I expect a lot more from you. You and Mr. Johnson can join me in detention tomorrow lunchtime and explain why you think that such stupidity and child-like behavior would ever make a good story."

Kate didn't know what to do; she had never had a detention before, ever. She didn't even hear the bell ring until Alek and Li started pulling her out the door and toward the secret RBI base. "So, which clue did you link the book to?" Kobe asked Kate when the agents had all gathered in the secret RBI base together.

Kate quickly walked around the lab, picking up all the clue tins they had found so far and emptied them on the desk together. She put

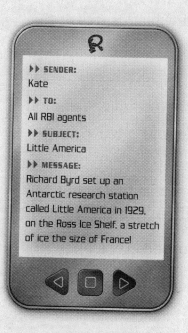

SENDER:
Kate

TO:
All RBI agents

SUBJECT:
Little America

MESSAGE:
Richard Byrd set up an Antarctic research station called Little America in 1929, on the Ross Ice Shelf, a stretch of ice the size of France!

the book down next to them.

"The book was about an explorer called Richard Byrd," she told the others as she went. "Do you remember the message I sent you? He spent a lot of time exploring Antarctica and set up a research station there called 'Little America'."

"Like the name of the hotel on the luggage label clue we found," said Jack.

Kate nodded, the luggage label in her hand.

"We need to go to that hotel," said Kobe.

"Wait a minute," said Zia. She walked over and picked up the original clue that had set them on this quest: the photo of Rip in the snow. "That luggage label has a penguin on it." She pointed to a tiny black speck at the side of the picture. "I've said since day one that *that* is a penguin."

The agents all leaned in toward the photo, squinting to try to make out what the tiny shape was.

"There's one way to settle this," said Li, appearing with a magnifying glass. She held it up to the photo and, sure enough, the little black speck took on the form of a penguin.

"But we know that it can't be a penguin," said Jack. "They live at the South Pole and this is obviously the North Pole, because the Northern Lights are in the sky."

"I've thought about that," said Zia. "What if they are not the Northern Lights? What if they are the Aurora Australis, the Southern Lights? They are exactly the same as the Northern Lights, but they appear in the southern hemisphere."

The other agents nodded at the possibility. Zia was the weather and geography expert, and if anyone knew about these things, then it would be her.

"So that's three of the clues we've linked,"

Li summarized. "What about this one?" She picked up the small carved whale.

"Whales live in the Antarctic," suggested Jack.

"Also, the explorer's Little America station was in an area of the Antarctic called the Bay of Whales," said Kate. "The whale could be a reference to that."

"So, do you think we need to go to Antarctica?" asked Alek.

"The clues seem to be pointing us in that direction," said Kate.

"But what about this?" asked Max, holding up the food order, the clue they had found on their trip to Japan. "I know the food on it is frozen, but it doesn't really tell us anything."

"I really don't know," said Kate. "Maybe it will make sense later. Perhaps—" Kate stopped as Mr. Cain walked into the lab—their teacher did not look to be in a good mood.

2

Antarctic Adventure

"I've just had an interesting conversation with Mr. Willis," said Mr. Cain, his normally happy face now frowning. Immediately, Kate forgot all the excitement about Antarctica and remembered her detention.

"I'm so sorry, Sir," she began. Seeing her RBI mission leader looking so disappointed in her was more than Kate could bear. "I was just so wound up about the clues, I had to tell Li. I know it was stupid to write anything down, but I didn't mention the RBI and—"

Mr. Cain held his hand up to silence Kate.

"I don't think the note Mr. Willis showed me had anything to do with the RBI or clues," he said.

"What do you mean, sir?" Kate asked, confused. "The note said that I had linked the book to another clue."

"Not the note I was shown." Mr. Cain rubbed his forehead as if he had a headache coming on. "This was an altogether different note."

"But—" Kate tried to think through what could have happened. "If that was a completely different note, then what happened to my note?"

"I might have ... eaten it," said Jack, sheepishly.

"What do you mean?" asked Kate.

"Well, when I saw Mr. Willis had noticed that Max had the note, I quickly got it back from him and, well, I did what I could to destroy the evidence."

"I didn't think the note could possibly have been anything to do with you, Kate," said Mr. Cain.

"So whose note was it then?" asked Kate, now worried about the note she had claimed as her own.

"Um, it was mine," Max replied.

Kate felt the worry turn to panic as she thought of all the things Max might have written.

"I thought it might be," said Mr. Cain.

"What did the note say?" asked Kate. "What did I tell Mr. Willis I wrote?"

"Mr. Willis stinks," said Max, proudly. Kate's heart sank.

"I'm going to kill you!" she shouted, as she tried to lunge across the table toward Max. Alek grabbed Kate around the waist, holding her back.

"Sir, we think we've solved the clues," said Li, keen to change the subject.

"We think we know where Ripley hid the artifact," added Kobe.

As the teacher who coordinated the RBI missions, Mr. Cain knew all about Ripley's hidden artifacts. He listened carefully as the agents told him they had linked the clues together and found that they were pointing them toward a research station in Antarctica.

"Can we send a team to investigate it, please?" asked Alek.

"Well, I'm not sure," said Mr. Cain. "It's not really investigating anything for the database, is it?" He rubbed his head again. "But then it is researching something for Rip."

"I think I might be able to help there." RIPLEY, the holographic head that was the team's link to the Ripley's database, appeared. "Over the last year or so, I have received reports from the Antarctic of somebody or something that doesn't look like an animal but has the ability to survive in the freezing icy temperatures of the Antarctic. This "thing" has been seen swimming alongside whales and seals in open water and beneath the ice. If you fell into the water there you would die in a matter of minutes because

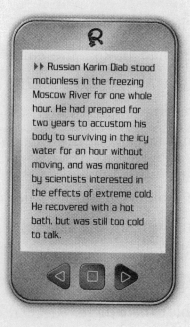

▶▶ Russian Karim Diab stood motionless in the freezing Moscow River for one whole hour. He had prepared for two years to accustom his body to surviving in the icy water for an hour without moving, and was monitored by scientists interested in the effects of extreme cold. He recovered with a hot bath, but was still too cold to talk.

of the cold. These sightings have filtered through, one at a time, so they haven't registered as something urgent that we should look into, but now seems like an excellent time."

"Can we go now we have a mission?" asked Li, hopefully.

"I don't see why not," Mr. Cain told her. "I'll contact someone at one of the research stations there and tell them to expect you. RIPLEY, tell us more."

"Well," the hologram began, "the reports say that this creature swims in the waters around Antarctica in virtually nothing."

"So?" asked Jack. "I used to go for a dip off

the coast back home in just my swimmers all the time."

"The waters around Australia's Gold Coast are about 80°F," RIPLEY explained. "The water in Antarctica is about 28°F."

"Wow," said Jack.

"I used to go ice swimming back in Russia," said Alek. "With ice swimming, you usually only stay in the water for about five minutes, don't you?" asked RIPLEY. "But only with weeks of training," Alek said.

"Well, one of the sightings you are going to investigate put this creature in the water for over two hours," RIPLEY told the amazed agents.

"I think that your ice swimming experience has just won you a place on the investigating team, Alek," said Mr. Cain. "It is going to be very cold there and any understanding of that at all will be a big help to your team."

He then turned to Kate. "As you are the one

who's read the book on this explorer and his ice station, I think you should also go," he added. "You know the most about it all. And it only seems fair, seeing as you made the first link between the clues."

The other agents all looked at their teacher, hoping that their skills might win them the final place on the team. Mr. Cain sighed before making his selection.

"Max," he said at last. "I hope I don't regret this decision, but you will be the third member of the team."

"Alright!" shouted Max.

"I am sending you because I think that your computer skills might be needed. If I'm right, the Little America research station has not been used for about 50 years, so some of its old research equipment might not be too keen to wake up. However, I do not want to hear of arguing between you and Kate on this mission, is that understood?"

Max nodded, still grinning.

"I'll make sure of it, Sir," said Kate, throwing Max a warning look.

"Thanks for making me the referee, Sir," said Alek, as he quickly followed the other two, who were already bickering, toward Dr. Maxwell's lab.

"Can't the rest of us go?" asked Kobe, the disappointment at not being chosen clear in his voice.

"I have another mission that I am going to need the rest of you for," said Mr. Cain. "RIPLEY, can you pull up the file for those reports we've had in from Egypt."

"Of course," said RIPLEY as the big view screen flickered into life in front of the remaining agents.

"Oh, wait a minute Kate," Mr. Cain called after them. Kate, Max, and Alek all turned around. "Are you sure that you can't link that food list?"

Kate shook her head. "It just doesn't seem to fit."

"It must," he said, studying the list in his hand. He folded it up and held it out to the group. Alek, who was closest, took it.

"Perhaps you should take it with you," Mr. Cain suggested. "You might find out how it links later."

"Thanks," said Alek, who really couldn't see what the food list had to do with anything. Maybe someone had found the tin before them and swapped that clue—DUL, the rival agency who always tried to stop the RBI, could be trying to throw them off the scent, perhaps? But then DUL didn't know about the artifact hunt, did they? Alek put the list in his pocket anyway. One thing he had learned from being part of the RBI was always to expect the unexpected!

Snow-skis

As the agents arrived at Dr. Maxwell's lab, they found him on what at first glance looked like a unicycle. However, as they looked more closely, the agents saw that the device actually had two wheels, side by side.

"What are you doing?" asked Max.

"I'm testing this," the professor explained. "It's an electric motorbike. It was sent to me by someone who thinks it is worthy of an entry in the Ripley's database, so I'm checking it out."

"Isn't that our job?" asked Alek.

Dr. Maxwell was the only other teacher in

the school who knew about the RBI. He always helped the agents with the equipment they would need for their latest missions, but Alek wasn't sure he liked the idea of the professor doing their work for them. What would be next, Mr. Cain coming on missions with them? The last thing the agents needed was teachers getting in their way.

"I'm not going to let you have all the fun, now am I?" Dr. Maxwell replied with a grin.

"Wow, can I have a turn?" asked Max.

"Later," the professor told him, stepping down from the bike. "Right now, I have gadgets to give you. Where are you going today?"

The agents filled Dr. Maxwell in on the morning's events and told him that they now needed to go to Antarctica.

"Then the first thing you will need are Antarctic dry suits," said Dr. Maxwell, handing the agents all-in-one black suits.

"Are they like wetsuits?" asked Kate.

"A bit," said Dr. Maxwell, "but they don't let any water in. They contain the latest thermal technology and should keep you warm in temperatures down to −40°F."

"RIPLEY said the water only got to 28°F," said Max.

"Ah yes, but you can wear these on land too, where the wind can lower the temperatures to far below zero," the professor explained, "and although the water isn't as cold as the wind, it will lower your body temperatures faster and that is what is most dangerous."

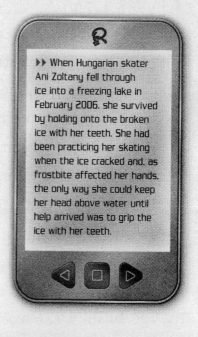

▶▶ When Hungarian skater Ani Zoltany fell through ice into a freezing lake in February 2006, she survived by holding onto the broken ice with her teeth. She had been practicing her skating when the ice cracked and, as frostbite affected her hands, the only way she could keep her head above water until help arrived was to grip the ice with her teeth.

"But we'll be safe in these, right?" asked Max.

"It would still be best to stay out of the water," Dr. Maxwell advised. "There's no way the suit will help protect you from the shock that hits your system as your body is surrounded by freezing water. Alek, with your ice swimming experience, the suit might help protect you for a bit longer, but none of you should be in the water for longer than five minutes."

He disappeared into a cupboard and then came out again with a strange gun-like object.

"This is an ice gun," he told the agents.

"Cool," said Max, reaching for it.

"It is to help you climb. The gun shoots a screw into the ice that has a rope attached to it. Or you can just use the screws as hand holds."

"How does it work?" asked Max, examining the gun.

"Careful—" Dr. Maxwell started, as Max's finger found the trigger and a screw shot out of the gun, burying itself in a wall of the laboratory, narrowly missing Alek.

"Oops," said Max.

Dr. Maxwell took the gun from Max and handed it to Alek.

"As the archery expert of the group, maybe you should look after this," he said. "Now, for your final gadget, follow me." Dr. Maxwell led them out of the lab and back into the main briefing room.

"I've been hoping to have some reason to use these for a long time," he explained, switching

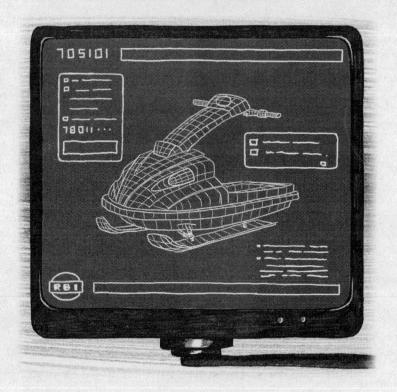

on the view screen and pressing some buttons. Immediately, the screen filled with an image.

"Snow-skis," Dr. Maxwell announced, proudly. "They'll be waiting for you when you arrive in Antarctica."

"Wow, snowmobiles," said Max, looking at the 3D image spinning slowly on the screen.

"No, not snowmobiles, snow-skis," Dr.

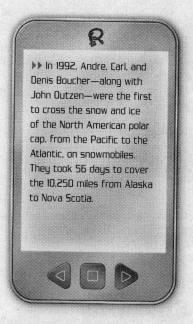

▶▶ In 1992, Andre, Carl, and Denis Boucher—along with John Outzen—were the first to cross the snow and ice of the North American polar cap, from the Pacific to the Atlantic, on snowmobiles. They took 56 days to cover the 10,250 miles from Alaska to Nova Scotia.

Maxwell corrected him. "Snowmobiles work with chains and tracks. These snow-skis act more like jet skis. They push the snow out behind you so you can go a lot faster, and they work easily on either snow or ice. They're all my own invention."

The sleek snow-skis looked like something Max couldn't wait to try!

Blinding Blizzards

"Do you think the snow-skis are here yet?" asked Max, as the agents arrived in Antarctica. "Where do you think they are?"

Max had been incredibly excited for the whole journey, and both Alek and Kate were beginning to get sick of the snow-skis before they had even seen them.

A scientist named Dr. Booth, who had been contacted by Mr. Cain, had greeted the agents.

Dr. Booth was now leading them back to the science camp, where he and the other scientists worked.

"Your teacher told us that you were coming out here, hoping to find the Little America station," he said.

"We think something that belongs in our school was lost there a long time ago and we want to find it so we can take it back to Ripley High," Kate explained.

"Well, I'm not sure when you'll be able to get out there," said Dr. Booth. "The remains of the last Little America station are on the other side of the ice shelf. It will take you a long time to get there, and there's a blizzard due to hit later today. It's not safe to be out there when the weather is so changeable."

"It won't take us long with our snow-skis!" Max insisted. "We'll get there and back before that blizzard comes anywhere near."

"Before we go," said Kate. "Have you heard anything about a man who swims in the sea here?"

Dr. Booth laughed. "You'd have to be pretty mad to do that!" he said. "There is a legend about a scientist who was working here long before I arrived. The story goes that he came here to study seals, but he was here for too long."

The agents looked at each other, unsure what this meant.

"I'm quite used to my home here, now," Dr. Booth explained. "But it's not always a pleasant place to live. People come and go, usually every six months, and rarely

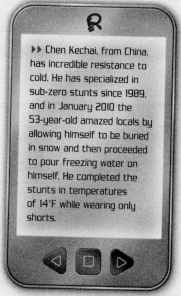

▶▶ Chen Kechai, from China, has incredible resistance to cold. He has specialized in sub-zero stunts since 1989, and in January 2010 the 53-year-old amazed locals by allowing himself to be buried in snow and then proceeded to pour freezing water on himself. He completed the stunts in temperatures of 14°F while wearing only shorts.

stay more than a year or so. This scientist began

to cut himself off from the others, and long periods of time alone in this wilderness can do funny things to your mind. People say that he went a bit crazy and started to think that he was one of the seals." Dr. Booth shrugged. "I think it's just a story, none of us have ever seen him. But you never know. He might still be out there, swimming with the seals."

Soon, the RBI agents were roaring across the ice shelf on their snow-skis. They had put the coordinates for the Little America station into the GPS feature on their R-phones, and were now following the directions.

"I think the snow's getting worse," shouted Kate over the howl of the wind. "That blizzard must have arrived earlier than expected."

"I can hardly hear you," called Alek. "Use the radio-mic in your hood."

Kate did as Alek suggested, switching to the small RBI-issue radio microphones built into the linings of their coats.

"I think the blizzard is here," said Max very loudly into his microphone. The other two winced at the volume. "What did they call it?"

"Katabatic winds," shouted Kate. "They're the winds blowing down from the higher points. They pick up the snow and the freezing air as they go and it just makes them colder."

"I can't see anything ahead apart from my snow-ski light," said Max.

"Neither can I," said Alek. "Perhaps we should turn back?"

"No, we can't," Kate urged. "We must be nearly there now. It will take us longer to get back than it will to get there."

"But where are we 'getting' to?" asked

▶▶ A "Williwaw" is a type of katabatic wind that forms around the Antarctic mountains and carries loose snow and ice down to the sea. These winds reach incredible speeds of 200 miles an hour very suddenly and can destroy buildings in their path. The fiercest regular winds on Earth, they are a great threat to boats off the coast and can last for days at a time.

Alek. "Dr. Booth said that there's nothing really out there."

Kate didn't say anything; she was hoping that Dr. Booth was wrong. She really wanted to see the research station she had read so much about in her book.

"I'm with Kate," said Max. "We should carry on."

Kate was more than a little surprised to hear Max agreeing with her, but she knew that he really wanted to find Rip's hidden artifact. Max powered his snow-ski forward ahead of the other two.

"Okay then," Alek agreed, speeding up to match Max's pace, the snow flying up out of the back of their snow-skis like a fountain.

The blizzard was against them and snow was flying directly into the agents' faces.

Then Max's snow-ski began to make a strange noise.

"I don't like the sound of that," he said. "It sounds like something is not coping too well in this blizzard."

"Can you fix it?" asked Kate.

"Not in this weather and not while we're moving," Max explained. His snow-ski light blinked on and off a couple of times before

the light died completely and the snow-ski stopped still.

"Well, you're not moving now," Alek pointed out.

"If we could find some shelter, then I could fix it," said Max.

"We have to hope that we find the station soon, then," said Alek.

He tied Max's snow-ski to the back of his own. "Jump on and share with Kate," he instructed. "I'll drag your snow-ski."

Max did as he was told and jumped up behind Kate, who did not look too happy to be sharing her snow-ski, and they started on their way again. It wasn't long before Alek's snow-ski started to make the same noise Max's had.

"Pulling the other snow-ski has worn out the engine," Max told Alek.

"I think we should call for help," suggested Kate.

Alek looked at his R-phone, but the blizzard

seemed to be blocking any signal.

"We can't," he told them. "The R-phones are being affected by the storm."

Kate's snow-ski began to sputter and Alek's stopped altogether.

"What are we going to do?" asked Max.

"I don't know," said Kate.

"You have to know!" Max told her. "You're the smart one, you always know what to do."

"Not this time," Kate shook her head.

The three RBI agents looked at each other through the snow, worried that they were going to be stranded in this freezing wilderness with no hope of rescue.

Ghost Station

"Wait," called Kate, squinting into the distance while trying to shield her face from the snow that was hitting her cheeks. "I can see something glinting out there. What is that?"

The others looked and could also just make out something reflecting the weak sunlight and gleaming amid the whiteness.

"Maybe it's yet another really big piece of ice," suggested Max, glumly.

"Or maybe it's the station," said Alek. He looked at his R-phone. Although he still had no signal, the GPS map was exactly as it was when he had set it. "We should be just about there."

The three agents pushed on through the snow, dragging their suffering snow-skis with them. As they drew nearer, the reflective surface turned out to be part of a large dome.

"It's the weather dome," said Kate, happily. "The research stations all had these round tops. We've found it!"

Alek quickly began scraping snow away from the tower and the areas around it until finally a door appeared. All three of the agents heaved until it opened and they hurried inside.

The station was pitch black. It was so covered in snow that no light at all was able to get in. Alek tried his flashlight, but the storm had taken its toll on it and the light sparked for just a second before going dark again. The room smelled stale and he reminded himself that no one had been inside this station since the 1960s.

"I think I've found the circuit box," said Max, feeling his way along the wall. "It won't be long now."

Alek smiled in the darkness. He couldn't see his hand in front of his face, but Max had somehow managed to find the power supply for the whole station.

Suddenly, there was light. Dim at first, as the old bulbs struggled to wake up from their long sleep, but then the room was bathed in a soft yellow glow.

"Well, they're nowhere near as good as the LED lights in the RBI base," said Max, eyeing the yellow lights suspiciously. "But they're not bad, considering how old they are."

"Go, Max!" said Alek. Although he was aware of everyone's special abilities in the RBI, it always amazed him when they were able to do things so well. "How did you do that so fast?" he asked Max.

"I do it all the time," Max replied casually. "I'm always looking for things to power the robots I invent and Dr. Maxwell's lab often has broken batteries or power units lying around—especially if Zia's been there!"

Alek laughed and decided that the others must all perfect their special talents, too, without him realizing.

"It's spooky," said Kate, as she wandered around the room. "It looks like a ghost town."

The station looked as if it had been abandoned in a hurry. There were still tables with chairs not pushed in, as if the person sitting in them might return at any moment, and desks with papers on them that might be needed for important research. The air in here was almost as cold as it had been outside. Although the agents were shielded from the wind, the outside temperatures had seeped into the building long ago, taking away any warmth that the RBI could have hoped to find.

"I'm going to see if I can fix the snow-skis," said Max, pulling out the RBI-issue toolkit that he always kept on his body somewhere.

"We should start looking for the artifact," suggested Kate, rubbing her gloved hands together to keep them warm.

"But where?" asked Max.

"Everywhere, I suppose."

Kate began moving around the room, lifting things, moving things, looking inside things.

Alek took a moment to collect his thoughts before diving in to help them. After all, they might not even know if they found the object—they had no idea what it was. There was a nagging thought in the back of his mind; something he knew would help, but he just couldn't remember it. He put his hand in his pocket and felt some paper there, when a shout from Kate made him jump.

"It can't be! It's just not possible!" she cried.

Alek and Max ran over to look at a plaque she had found, just visible near the far station wall.

'LITTLE AMERICA V' read the top line in bold capitals. Underneath, in smaller,

more ornate script, was written "established 1955."

"Oh," said Max, understanding. "This station was built six years after Rip's death."

"So there's no way he could have left an artifact here," Kate added.

"Maybe he got someone else to do it," suggested Max. "That explorer guy from your book—it was his station after all."

"No," said Kate, certain he was wrong. "Rip set up all those clues himself. How could he have done that after he died? Besides, you read the note—Rip had to hide these artifacts, things weren't safe. DUL was looking for them."

"Maybe it was his ghost," said Max.

"Ssh, a minute and stop being silly," Kate snapped. "I'm trying to think." She looked again at the plaque. "Oh, I've been so foolish! It's the station that's a ghost. Max, what does that top line say?"

"Little America V," he read.

"No," Kate told him. "Not 'V', five! 'V' is the Roman numeral for five! This is the fifth Little America station. We need to look for one of the older ones that would have been here when Rip visited."

"And where do we find those?" asked Alek.

"The book said that all the Little America research stations where built around the same area," Kate explained. "It must be near here somewhere."

"Well, we're lucky," said Alek, sticking his head out the station door. "The blizzard has stopped and it's a lot easier to see now."

The three agents crept outside, their eyes dazzled by the sun reflecting off the snow—a bright contrast to the dull glow of the lights inside the old station.

"We're very close to the edge of the ice shelf," said Alek. "We need to be careful. Pieces of ice can just break off and float away with no warning. We should stick together and keep as far away from the edge as we can." Alek had spent a lot of time training in extremely cold places and knew the dangers that hid in frozen landscapes.

▶▶ After more than 100 penguins were left stranded on beaches in Rio de Janeiro, Brazil, in 2006, the Brazilian air force and navy transported them safely back to Antarctica. Penguins arrive from the Antarctic on ice floes that melt near Brazil's coast every winter, and the flightless birds then find themselves washed up on Rio's beaches.

The others nodded and moved away from where the sea was hitting the smooth ice edge of the land.

"There are lots of other dangers while we're walking around out here," Alek began to explain. "You really have to watch every step or—"

He was cut off as Kate found out what he meant. She placed her foot on what she thought was solid snow, only to have it disappear beneath her. The ice opened up, revealing a jagged hole in the landscape, and Kate went tumbling down into a deep, dark crevasse.

Crevasse Climbing

Max couldn't believe his eyes as, with lightning speed, Alek leaped into the crevasse after Kate. Slightly stunned, he leaned over the edge to watch. He couldn't understand how jumping in after Kate would help. He just knew that he had two friends in there now and wondered how he could get help. He looked into the yawning, dark crevasse. It was so deep that he couldn't see the bottom. However, what he did see surprised him: it looked like his friends had stopped falling part way down.

Alek thought fast as he saw Kate disappearing into the gaping black hole. As he dove after her, he had fired the ice gun, sending a screw into the solid wall of ice. He had then let the rope attached to the screw play out.

Alek streamlined his body to increase the speed of his descent and it wasn't long before he caught up to her. He quickly reached out and grabbed his friend, pulling her close to him as the rope snapped taut. The two agents were left hanging, Alek with his arm up above his head gripping the rope, and Kate clinging to him, finding it hard to believe she had stopped falling.

"Are you okay?" Max's voice echoed off the sheer walls as he shouted down to them.

Alek looked up to see Max as a faint silhouette up above.

"I think so," he shouted back.

"What can I do?" asked Max.

"Just stay well back so that you don't fall in too," said Alek. "The edges could still crumble."

Max took a big step back away from the crevasse.

"Are you all right?" Alek asked Kate, who

had said nothing since he had caught her. She looked up at him and nodded.

"Just a little shocked," she said.

"I need you to climb onto my back," he said.

Kate carefully maneuvered herself so that she was behind him, with her legs wrapped around his waist and her arms clinging to his neck.

"Can you loosen your grip just a bit?" asked Alek, coughing.

"Sorry," she said, relaxing her hold and grasping his shoulders instead.

"Now hold on tight," he told her.

Alek stretched out his arms and legs so that they were touching the narrow walls of the crevasse. He shuffled his hands up a couple of inches and then his feet so that he was walking spider-like up the sheer sides. As they climbed further up the crevasse, it opened out more and Alek was no longer able to reach both sides.

▶▶ When British climber Joe Simpson broke his leg on a snow-covered mountain in Peru, in 1985, his partner was forced to save himself by cutting the 330-foot rope that was holding Simpson above a large crevasse. Simpson miraculously survived the drop, and crawled 5½ miles back to base camp. His experience was made into a book and a film.

Instead, he gripped the rope attached to the ice screw and pulled them both up using that.

When they reached the top, Alek climbed out and landed in the soft snow that had hidden the crevasse earlier. Kate released her grip on him and scrambled away from the edge.

Max ran over and hugged both of them.

"Thanks," Kate said to Alek. "I didn't think I was getting out of that one."

Alek just nodded, still getting his breath back.

"I thought I was going to be stuck here all by myself," said Max. "Mr. Cain would have killed me if I'd lost you both at once!"

Alek playfully punched Max on the shoulder; he could see in his friend's eyes that Max had been worried.

As the agents walked back to the station Max noticed his R-phone buzz back to life.

"I think we should call back to the RBI base if the phones are working," said Kate. "It's too dangerous to carry on like this with no coordinates." She looked at Alek. "And next time something happens you might not be able to save me!"

Max called the number programmed into his R-phone that would get them a direct line to RIPLEY. When the phone connected to the hologram's interface, Max put it on speaker so the others could hear.

Kate explained that the station they had found was the fifth Little America research base and that they needed an earlier station.

"Can you give us the coordinates for it please,

RIPLEY?" she asked.

"I can, but I'm not sure it will be of much use," RIPLEY told her. "The older Little America stations were all lost."

"What do you mean?" asked Alek.

"The stations were built on a piece of ice that broke away from the mainland in 1987."

"You mean it became an iceberg?" asked Alek. "Won't it have melted by now?"

"I am looking up the course of that particular iceberg now," RIPLEY told them. "Some icebergs drift away from the Antarctic and end up in warmer waters, where they dissolve quite quickly. Your iceberg, however, known as B9, seems to have stayed quite close to home."

The agents looked at each other, pleased with this news.

"It was caught by strong currents, which trapped it nearby. In 1989, B9 had a major collision with the ice shelf and broke into three parts. The smallest was still over

50 miles across, which is four times longer than Manhattan Island in New York."

"Which part do we need?" asked Max. "Unfortunately, I can't tell you that," said RIPLEY. "My data can track the course of the iceberg, and the three smaller ones it became, but there is no information about what you might find in any of those bergs."

▶▶ New icebergs float off from the main Antarctic ice shelf on a regular basis. In 2005, an iceberg the size of Dallas broke from Antarctica, and, in 2000, an iceberg known as B15, thought to be the biggest ever recorded at over 183 miles long—bigger than Jamaica—made its way across the Ross Sea. It was so large that parts of it have still not melted.

"Great," said Max. "What are we going to do?"

"You will just have to search all three until you find the right one," RIPLEY told him.

"RIPLEY, I don't think that's going to be possible," said Alek. "Even with Dr. Maxwell's super-protective dry suits, the cold water will be too much. I've just climbed up a sheer ice face, and my hands are pretty cold. I don't think I could manage to climb all over an iceberg, and certainly not three!"

"You climbed an ice face?" asked RIPLEY, concerned.

"It's a long story," said Alek, quickly. "Just know it's not something I want to do again!"

"How are you getting on with the other mission?" asked RIPLEY.

Kate told RIPLEY about the legend of the scientist who went to live with the seals.

"I'd suggest investigating that first," said RIPLEY. "If you can find that scientist, he might be able to help you."

Dangerous Discoveries

After speaking to RIPLEY, they had returned to the abandoned station and Max had fixed the snow-skis. Now they were as good as new again. Max had set the coordinates RIPLEY had given them into his R-phone and less than half an hour later, the agents were back on their snow-skis and headed toward the area where the scientist had been based.

"What's that over there?" said Alek, pointing to a small structure in the snow.

As the agents approached, they saw it was a small wooden hut. It looked like an old outhouse that might have been used for storage for one of the larger research stations. There was a small window, and someone had hung curtains on it.

Kate knocked on the door. The agents waited, but there was no answer.

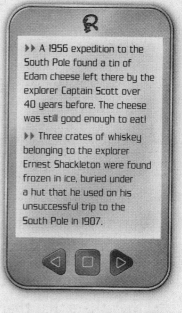

▶▶ A 1956 expedition to the South Pole found a tin of Edam cheese left there by the explorer Captain Scott over 40 years before. The cheese was still good enough to eat!

▶▶ Three crates of whiskey belonging to the explorer Ernest Shackleton were found frozen in ice, buried under a hut that he used on his unsuccessful trip to the South Pole in 1907.

"Maybe it's just an old storage building," said Alek "Perhaps there never was any scientist."

"A storage hut with curtains?" said Max. "I don't think so."

"Or the scientist could have died a long time ago," suggested Kate. "I can't imagine life would be easy, being out here all by yourself."

Max turned the door handle.

"It's open," he told the others, as he walked in.

"Max, wait," said Kate. "We can't just go in. This could be someone's home! Or worse, it could be dangerous."

But Max was already inside. He stuck his head back out the door.

"Are you coming?" he asked.

Kate and Alek looked at each other. Alek shrugged and followed Max into the hut. Kate was right behind him.

The hut had been made into a small cabin. There was a little stove where a pot sat over a fire grate. Alek held his hand toward it and told the others that there had been a fire there recently. Max ran a finger around the edge of the pot, before putting it in his mouth.

"Mmm, fish stew," he said. "And still warm."

"So someone definitely has been here recently," said Kate. "But where are they now?"

"These coordinates are exactly where RIPLEY said the creature had last been," said Max double checking the readings. "Perhaps he really is human and this is his house. Maybe he went for a swim. Isn't that what he does? We should go take a look."

"As long as we're careful," said Alek. The agents walked along the Antarctic coast, trying to see if they could spot anyone swimming.

"Ooh, I can see some penguins," said Max. "Jack asked if I'd get some photos for him. He's hoping I'd find some rare ones, I think."

Max started to run off in the direction of the penguins, his R-phone in his hand as he set it to camera mode. Alek started to go after him, when suddenly Kate shouted.

"There's something over there," she said, pointing in the opposite direction. Alek could see something by the edge of the ice.

"Be careful, Max," Alek shouted to his friend, who was skidding over the ice and launching himself at the poor penguins. The birds tried to scatter as Max headed toward them. Alek thought it was funny that these penguins probably weren't used to people, but still knew

enough to be scared of the loud boy heading toward them with a flashing camera.

Alek, however, went after Kate. She might have found something important and after her slip in the crevasse earlier, he decided that it was she who probably needed keeping an eye on most. He found her holding what looked like a leather jacket.

"I think this coat is made out of seal skins," she said.

"It would have been a pretty big seal," Alek smiled. "You'd have to check with Jack, but I don't think they get that big."

"It's several skins sewn together by hand," said Kate. "I think we might have found our man."

They both looked out into the waters nearby, trying to see anything that might look like a person, but a loud shout caught their attention.

"That's Max," said Kate.

Alek was already running back toward the group of penguins, but saw Max was no longer there.

"Oh, my goodness," said Kate, catching up and spotting Max.

The Antarctic coastline is forever changing, with small pieces of ice breaking away all the time. While trying to get a photo of the penguins, Max had moved closer to the edge of

the ice than he really should have. A small piece had come loose while he was standing on it and was now floating away from the mainland.

"Help!" he yelled.

Alek grabbed the ice gun and shot it in the direction of the floating ice. A screw buried itself in the ice and the tiny ice island was then tied to the mainland by the rope attached to the screw.

Max breathed a sigh of relief as he felt his island stop moving.

"Hang on," called Alek. He pulled the rope tight and began to reel it in, hand over hand, slowly pulling the tiny ice island toward him.

Max felt himself moving slowly toward the mainland. However, the movement began to change. The whole ice island jerked suddenly and he fell forward on to his hands and knees, his head right above the ice screw. He could see that large cracks were forming all around it and reaching out under his feet.

"Stop!" he shouted to Alek. "The ice is cracking!"

The force of the screw hitting the block of ice had made it start to crumble. The whole piece of ice was about to fall apart and the ice screw was very close to slipping out, setting Max on a course out into the Atlantic Ocean.

Ice Man

"I'll swim over and get him," said Alek, unzipping his coat.

"No," said Kate. "There's no point in both of you getting wet and cold. Max is a good swimmer, he can swim across by himself."

Alek nodded, seeing the sense in Kate's suggestion.

"Max, you're going to have to swim back to us," Alek shouted to him.

"But what about the current?" asked Max, looking at the water whipping by his feet. "It's quite strong; it will pull me off course."

"Use the rope," suggested Alek. "It will guide you across."

"You'll have to hurry though," said Kate, looking at the screw wobbling in the ice.

"Put your hood up," Alek suggested.

Max pulled up the hood on the dry suit, and jumped into the water. As the cold water hit him, it was like nothing he had ever experienced. For a moment, he found he was completely confused. It was as if his brain had just stopped working for a second or two. When it clicked back in, Max found that he was thrashing his arms around.

"The cold water can disorientate you," explained Alek from the shore. "His brain is trying to work out what's going on. Grab the rope, Max!"

Max heard Alek's shout and grabbed the rope

before the current pulled him away from it. He felt as if he had been hit by a train. All the air in his lungs seemed to have been driven out and he found himself gasping for breath.

"Make sure you keep your head above the water," shouted Alek, just as a huge wave washed over Max's head and he started coughing up ice-cold seawater.

Max shook his head, trying to get all his senses to work together and quickly began to make his way along the rope.

"That's it, Max," called Alek. He turned to Kate.

"That ice screw is looking really loose," she said, worry in her voice. "If he doesn't move quickly, it's going to come out completely."

"Not only that, but Max's body isn't used to these cold temperatures—his fingers will start to go numb fast and he could get hypothermia," Alek told her.

They looked back to see Max working his way steadily along the rope.

"He's doing really well," said Kate.

Suddenly, Max began to swerve off course.

"What happened?" asked Kate.

"The ice screw has come out!" said Alek. He could see the rope still in Max's hand, but now that it was no longer attached to the floating ice, it too was being pulled along by the current.

"What's going on?" shouted Max, his head bobbing in and out of the icy water.

"I'm going in to get him," said Alek. He took his shoes off so their weight wouldn't slow him down and threw them in a pile on the ground with his jacket.

"Wait, what's that?" asked Kate.

A pale shape appeared in the water next to Max and in an instant pulled him under. Alek tensed, ready to leap in and save Max but Kate grabbed his arm to stop him.

"Don't," she warned. "Something's in there."

"And it got Max, I have to help!" Alek exclaimed.

"If it got Max, it could get you too!" cried Kate, clinging tighter to Alek's arm so that he couldn't go in.

They watched the water where Max had vanished, hoping to see him appear again, but nothing happened. Then they heard coughing and spluttering from farther down the shore. The agents both turned quickly to see Max pulling himself out of the water.

They rushed over to him just as something else appeared from the water beside him. It was a man wearing only swimming trunks.

"Oh good, thank you for bringing my jacket,"

said the man, pointing to the seal skin that Kate was still carrying. "I think your friend here could use it." He started to pull Max out of his wet coat.

"Stop," said Kate. "Can't you see he's freezing?" She looked at Max, who was shivering with his teeth chattering loudly.

"We need to get him out of the wet clothes," the man explained. "They will only make him colder as the wind hits him."

Once Max was in just the dry suit he had been wearing under the wet clothes, the man took the seal skin from Kate and wrapped it around Max. Alek bundled his dry jacket around Max too.

▶▶ In cold water you will lose heat over 20 times faster than in air of the same temperature. It's actually a better idea to float than to swim in freezing water. Swimming encourages blood flow to your extremities, where it will lose body heat much faster. Wet clothing must be removed as quickly as possible to prevent hypothermia from setting in.

"We should get him in the warm," said the man. "Follow me."

"Should we go with him?" Kate asked Alek in a whisper. "He must be mad. He's been in that water in just his swimming trunks!"

"Believe it or not!" said Alek, smiling. "This is the man we've come to investigate. Of course we should follow him, we need to interview him for the database." He started to go after Max and the man.

Kate followed, still unsure.

They reached the wooden hut they had been in earlier, and the man lit a fire. He sat Max down by it and turned to the other agents.

"Your friend here had a lucky escape," he told them. "What are you doing all the way out here by yourselves?"

"We were looking for you," Alek told him, and then explained all about the RBI and the database.

The man listened carefully and then told them his story. His name was Felix Heller and he was a German scientist who had come to Antarctica over 30 years ago to study the life cycles and family patterns of seals. To begin with his results had been terrible, but he soon realized that the noise of the research base and its constantly changing people was quite frightening to the seals, who avoided the people as much as they could.

Then, slowly, as the ice in the area became less stable, with big cracks forming in it, people left the station and began to set up on the other side of the ice shelf, where Dr. Booth's research station was now. With fewer people, the seals were easier to study; they came close and began to relax into their natural habits. Eventually, everybody left until he was the only human there.

"Weren't you lonely?" asked Kate.

"Not at all," Felix told her. "I have always

quite liked my own company, and I have the seals. They let me swim and play with them and they treat me as one of their own. I find them a lot easier to live with than I did the other scientists!" He laughed at his joke and Alek realized that his laugh sounded a little like a seal's bark.

"But what about the cold?" he asked. "How are you able to swim in the water without thermal clothing?"

Felix shrugged. "I don't really know. I am just used to the cold. I slowly built up my ability to stand the cold with training over time. I need little more than these seal skins. I often swim in just my old swimming shorts. I go for long runs in them too."

"That's incredible," Alek told him, amazed. "I don't really understand how you survive the extreme cold, I wonder if RIPLEY can explain," he said, tapping into his R-phone as he spoke. He knew that the Antarctica marathon was considered one of the toughest in the world due to the difficulties of running in such cold temperatures, but Felix did it in just shorts! "There was another reason we came to Antarctica," Alek explained, "and you might just be able to help us."

"Of course," said Felix. "As much as I love my seal friends, it is nice to talk to somebody who doesn't bark!"

> ▸▸ **SENDER:** RIPLEY
> ▸▸ **SUBJECT:** Icy response
> ▸▸ **MESSAGE:**
> All mammals, including humans, have a "diving reflex," which automatically activates as soon as their faces are submerged in cold water. The heart rate slows and the blood vessels in the arms and legs tighten, to save blood for important organs. That cannot account for this extreme example however, he should be freezing!

Once Max had warmed up and the agents had recorded all the information on Felix that they would need for their database entry, they set off on their snow-skis back to the original research station. There they collected an inflatable

RBI-issue boat that they had brought with them on their mission and they now set out in it, first to pick up Felix and then to find the coordinates RIPLEY had given them for the icebergs.

"Wow, they are so beautiful," said Felix, as the three icebergs came into view.

"Which one should we start with?" asked Max, now back in his own jacket.

"The first one," said Felix. He borrowed an RBI-issue scuba breathing system and dove into the icy water as if it were the Ripley High School pool, then swam straight over to the huge block of floating ice.

"I'll be back in a minute," he called to the RBI agents, as he disappeared beneath the iceberg.

The agents watched as every so often Felix appeared on top of the iceberg or from a hole in the side, before disappearing again on his search. Finally, he appeared on the top and dove back into the water, swimming back to the boat.

"No luck," he said. "Let's move on to number two."

The agents were amazed that Felix still didn't seem to notice the cold at all. They brought the little boat around to the second iceberg, which Felix searched again, but found nothing, and then they moved on to the third one.

Ten minutes passed as Felix explored the

ice mountain.

"Could RIPLEY have given us the wrong coordinates?" asked Kate. "Perhaps these aren't the three icebergs we were looking for. Or maybe the part that the station was in melted and Little America is now buried at the bottom of the ocean?"

"RIPLEY is never wrong," said Max. "Besides, we can just get Felix to search the ocean floor next!"

"Do you know how deep the water here is?" asked Kate, annoyed with Max's relaxed attitude.

"Just chill," he told her, "It'll be fine."

Kate was not so sure, but then she was snapped out of her worry by a shout from the iceberg.

It was Felix—and he had found something. He was waving his hands very excitedly. The agents hurried over toward him eager to hear what he had found.

The Lost Artifact

Felix told the agents that he had discovered a building hidden in the iceberg. Alek brought the boat as close to the iceberg as he could and anchored it. The agents then used their ice guns to help them climb onto the ice and to the place where Felix was waiting for them. He led them through a tunnel carved deep in the ice to a door.

"It looks just like the door to the other

station," said Kate.

Alek opened it and the agents stepped through into the building on the other side.

Alek switched his flashlight on, which was now working again.

"Wow," said Kate. "It looks exactly like the other Little America station."

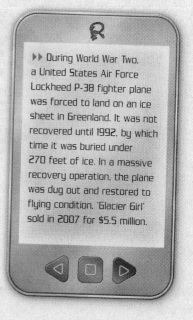

▶▶ During World War Two, a United States Air Force Lockheed P-38 fighter plane was forced to land on an ice sheet in Greenland. It was not recovered until 1992, by which time it was buried under 270 feet of ice. In a massive recovery operation, the plane was dug out and restored to flying condition. 'Glacier Girl' sold in 2007 for $5.5 million.

"Except it's sideways," added Max.

The station was an exact replica of Little America V, but Max was right. When the iceberg had broken away from the mainland, it had tipped on its side, and everything in the station was now at a strange angle. The station had been buried deep within the iceberg and had been floating inside it ever since.

"This is the station we've been looking for,"

said Max. "Let's start searching." Max began to rummage through anything he could find, looking for Rip's lost artifact.

Again, Alek tried to think of anything that would help narrow down their search area. He put his hand into his pocket and pulled out the piece of paper he had felt there earlier. He found he was looking at the food order list; the clue they hadn't been able to solve.

"What's that?" Kate asked.

Alek handed her the clue and she looked at it carefully. This clue had been bothering her. Kate was really good at solving puzzles and cryptic problems, but for some reason she had not been able to work out how the food list fitted in. However, now something clicked in her mind.

"Alek, you're a genius!" she exclaimed. "This list is the answer!"

The other agents and Felix looked at her.

"All of the other clues led us to this station,

right?" she asked.

The others nodded.

"But nothing told us where in the station we should look. So, this food list is an order form for frozen food. And where was food kept?"

"In a fridge!" said Max.

Kate rolled her eyes at him.

"Yes," she said, "but where would the fridge be?"

"In the kitchen," Alek replied.

"Right!" said Kate. "We just have to find the kitchen."

"I can help with that," said Felix. "The kitchen, or galley as we called it, would be this way." He walked carefully along the sharply sloping floor and the agents followed. Soon, they came to the edge. Everything further on was underwater. Part of a wall was sticking out of the water with the word "GALLEY" written on it.

"The galley is underwater, isn't it?" asked Max.

"What are we going to do?" asked Kate. She was beginning to feel the cold, trapped inside the iceberg, and she rubbed her hands together, trying to get some warmth.

"We'll have to go in," said Alek, looking at the water.

"I'm not going in that water again," Max shuddered.

"You won't have to," said Alek. "Felix and I will go."

"Are you sure you can handle the freezing water?" Felix asked Alek.

"I'm Russian," Alek told him. "I grew up swimming in freezing lakes."

Felix looked worried, but agreed that Alek could come with him.

As soon as Alek and Felix had put on the RBI-issue breathing masks, they were ready to go. Kate and Max stood well back from the edge of the water as Alek dove into it, following Felix.

Alek felt his body temperature drop instantly. He swam after Felix, who he could see kicking ahead with no problems. This water was much colder than anything he had ever felt before and trying to breathe underwater was harder. Alek was really struggling to make his lungs work properly. The air in the tanks was quickly getting too cold for him to take in.

Felix looked back and saw that Alek was in

trouble. He made large gestures for Alek to turn back. Alek was not a quitter and could happily say that he had never given up on anything in his life before, but he knew that carrying on would be a mistake. He reluctantly turned around and swam back to where Max and Kate were waiting.

His head broke the surface and Max helped him out of the freezing water.

"Oh my goodness, you look so pale!" said Kate.

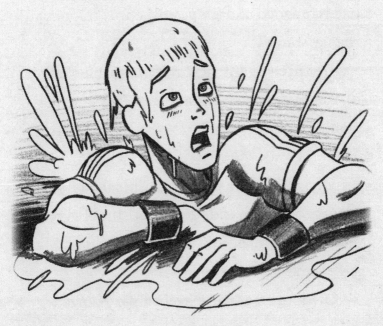

She rushed off and found an old blanket.

"What happened?" asked Max, but Alek's teeth were chattering too much to talk.

Alek sat down on the floor, his legs almost giving out under him, and let Kate wrap the blanket around him and rub his arms and legs, trying to get some heat back into them.

Five minutes passed, and there was no sign of Felix. Alek began to worry that he shouldn't have left him there alone. Perhaps something had happened and the scientist was trapped in the icy water?

The three agents sat watching the surface of the water, waiting and hoping that Felix would return.

Finally, there was a large splash as Felix emerged. He handed something to Kate and dried himself off on a blanket that Max gave him.

Kate looked at the extraordinary object.

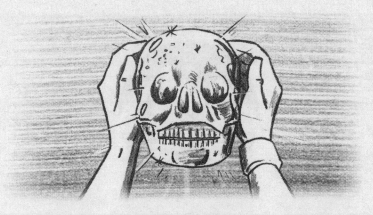

"Is that a skull?" asked Max.

"Yes, it is," said Kate. "I think we've found our missing artifact!" The agents crowded round her excitedly.

"It's amazing, but it looks as if it's made of glass. It can't be a human skull," Max said.

"No, it's not a human skull," said Kate, irritated by Max. "It's a crystal skull."

The others looked at the artifact spellbound by the light and reflections that almost blinded them—it almost looked as if it was alive! They could not wait to take it back to Ripley High to show the other agents.

Secret of the Crystal Skull

A week later, when the agents were back at Ripley High, the rest of the RBI were keenly examining the new artifact together.

"So, does this have magical powers?" asked Jack.

"I don't know," said Kate. "There are legends that tell of crystal skulls causing visions. Some people even say that they were created by aliens."

"Wow, aliens," said Max.

"So they can produce visions can they?" asked Kobe, taking the skull from Jack.

"I can feel Ripley and a native tribe. I think they're somewhere in South America," said Kobe, as his amazing ability gave him flashes of the skull's history. "But no aliens."

"There was a crystal skull found in Belize in the 1920s," said Kate. "It was said to be ancient Mayan, but many people think it's a fake."

"So how do we know if ours is the real deal?" asked Jack.

"I got an amazing feeling from it," said Kobe. "I don't think a fake would feel that special."

"Can I look at it?" asked Zia.

"Of course," said Max, handing her the skull. "There's no computer in it, as far as we know."

Zia pulled a face at Max and took the skull.

"It looks like it's been carved out of some form of quartz," she said. "But not one I've ever seen. It also looks as if the whole skull has been carved out of one piece of crystal and ... wait a minute."

Zia was holding the jaw, which suddenly moved in her hand.

"She's broken it!" cried Max.

"No, the skull found in Belize had a moveable jaw," said Kate.

"There's something loose in here," said Zia, as she carefully lowered the jaw and put her hand inside the mouth. She pulled out one of the teeth.

"Now she's really broken it!" shouted Max.

"No, I think there's something on this tooth," said Zia. "It's really tiny—so small I can't make out what it is."

"This might help," suggested Li as she handed Zia one of Rip's extraordinarily powerful magnifying glasses. "I use it for studying miniature art."

Zia looked through the magnifying glass

and saw that there was writing carved into
the tooth.

"I think it's a message from Rip," she told
the group.

"Read it then!" shouted Max.

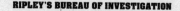

Congratulations!

You are true followers of the amazing and have achieved the impossible—you have found the first hidden artifact.

This crystal skull was discovered in Mexico and is thought to possess mystical powers. Before I could investigate this, I was forced to hide the skull. I could not risk it falling into the wrong hands ... I hope you will protect this artifact and find out its true powers.

Now the search is on for my next hidden treasure!

Ripley

Taking a deep breath Zia read the message to the group.

"Wow," said Kobe. "We did it!"

"Hang on, I think Zia's joking with us,"

said Max. "How could Rip have written all that on a tiny tooth?"

"That's nothing," said Li. "I can show you a grain of rice that has over 250 letters on it!"

"That's unbelievable, believe it or not!" said Jack.

▶▶ The 65 words—254 letters—of the Lord's Prayer have been inscribed on one single grain of rice! Rice writers were employed at the Ripley's odditoriums in the 1930s to produce grains to sell as souvenirs. This piece is thought to have been done by E.L. ("The Amazing") Blystone of Ardara, Pennsylvania. He used no form of magnification to work and his personal record was an amazing 1,615 letters on a single grain!

"So, what Rip is telling us is that there are more artifacts out there for us to find," added Kobe.

"What should we do first?" asked Jack.

"Max, you take the skull to Dr. Maxwell and see if he can find out anything about it," said Kobe. "I'm going to find a place to keep it."

"And we have a new adventure," said Kate, excitement in her voice.

"There are more hidden treasures out there for us to find," agreed Alek.

The agents looked at each other, wondering what other amazing things Rip had hidden somewhere, just waiting to be found.

Their next worldwide quest had only just begun!

RIPLEY'S DATABASE ENTRY

RIPLEY FILE NUMBER : 54763

MISSION BRIEF : Believe it or not, a man has been sighted swimming with seals in the freezing waters of Antarctica. Investigate accuracy of these accounts for Ripley database.

CODE NAME : Sub-zero Swimmer

REAL NAME : Felix Heller

LOCATION : Antarctica

AGE : 54

HEIGHT : 5 ft 7 in

WEIGHT : 160 lb

VIDEO CAPTURE

UNUSUAL CHARACTERISTICS :

Ability to swim in sub-zero waters wearing nothing more than swimming trunks. Is also able to exercise and run in freezing conditions without protective clothing.

RBI DATABASE APPROVED!

INVESTIGATING AGENTS :

Alek Filipov, Kate Jones, Max Johnson

▶▶ YOUR NEXT ASSIGNMENT

JOIN THE RBI IN THEIR NEXT ADVENTURE!

SHOCK HORROR

Prologue

"What was that?" asked Cara, sitting up suddenly in her sleeping bag.

"It was probably just a coyote," her friend Brinna told her as she rolled over and tried to stay asleep.

Cara strained to hear the noise again in the darkness. She was sure it wasn't a coyote. It sounded more like a crackle or a hiss.

"Can you smell smoke?" asked Brinna, suddenly awake now.

"Brinna, your hair!" As Cara looked at her friend, she could see Brinna's long, blond hair sticking to the side of the tent, pulled there by static electricity.

"Yuk," said Brinna, trying to pull her hair away from the fabric.

"There's that noise again," said Cara with a gasp.

"I heard it too," said Brinna, and this time she knew it wasn't a coyote. Something was out there. "I'm going out to see what it is." Brinna picked up her flashlight and unzipped the tent. She slowly stepped outside.

The forest was dark, Brinna shone her flashlight around but nothing seemed out of place. The hissing and crackling noises were louder now though.

"What can you see?" Cara stuck her head out of the tent to find out what was going on.

"There's nothing out here," Brinna told her. "But those noises have to be coming from somewhere." She took a couple steps away from the tent. "It certainly is a warm night." She wiped her forehead where beads of sweat were beginning to form. "I feel like I'm in a sauna."

As she moved farther into the forest, the darkness and the heat seemed smothering. Brinna felt as if the trees were closing in around her.

There was a noise to her right, a horrible screeching, screaming noise and suddenly a tree burst into flames.

Brinna jumped away and fell to the ground. A tree close to where she landed burst into flames just as the first one had done. Brinna quickly picked herself up and ran back toward the tent, trees exploding all around her.

"Run!" called Brinna as she reached the tent where Cara was waiting outside.

Cara's face was a mask of panic. She quickly started running and the two girls disappeared down the hillside as fast as they could.

▶▶

ENTER THE STRANGE WORLD OF RIPLEY'S...

▶▶ Believe it or not, there is a lot of truth in this remarkable tale. The Ripley's team travels the globe to track down true stories that will amaze you. Read on to find out about real Ripley's case files and discover incredible facts about some of the extraordinary people and places in our world.

Ripley's
Believe *It* or *Not!* ®

CASE FILE #001

▶▶ ICEMAN

Wim Hof from the Netherlands has the ability to perform extreme feats in freezing cold conditions.

▶▶ Wim swam for over 60 yards under thick ice on a lake in Finland in 2000.

▶▶ He completed a marathon in −4°F in 2009, wearing only shorts.

▶▶ In 2010, in Japan, Wim stood in an ice bath for 1 hour 44 minutes, breaking his own record.

▶▶ Wim says that he can make his body warm by using the power of his brain and ancient Tibetan meditation techniques.

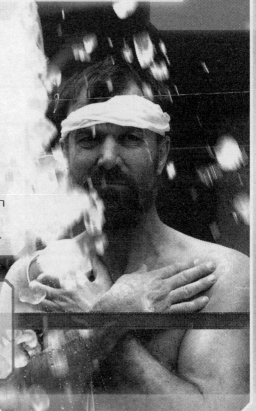

credit: Jeff Chen/Trigger Images

credit: © kkaplin/Fotolia.com

▶▶ The lowest temperature ever recorded on earth was at Lake Vostock, Antarctica, in 1983, where it dropped to –128°F.

▶▶ The area contains 90 percent of all ice in the world, and 68 percent of the fresh water in the world.

▶▶ Ridge A in Antarctica has an average temperature of –94°F, the coldest place in the world. It is unlikely that anyone has ever set foot there.

▶▶ The deepest point on land is the Bentley Trench, which lies under the ice of Antarctica. This depression is more than 8,200 feet below sea level.

▶▶ When Mount Erebus, Antarctica, erupts, it throws out pieces of pure gold in its volcanic lava.

▶▶ In 1915, pack ice trapped the ship *Endurance* as explorer Ernest Shackleton and 27 men attempted to cross Antarctica. They spent months stuck on drifting ice before making perilous voyages in open boats through some of the coldest and most stormy waters on Earth to find help. Shackleton eventually rescued the remaining members of his crew in August 1916. Over the entire ordeal, not a single life was lost.

CASE FILE #002

▶▶ CRYSTAL SKULLS

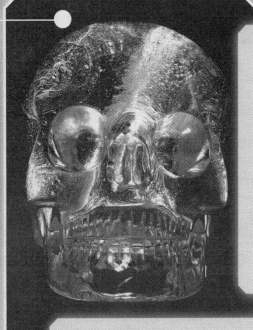

credit: AFP/Getty Images

This crystal skull was presented to a Paris museum by explorer Alphonse Pinart in 1878. It stands 4½ inches high and could be as much as 35,000 years old. No one knows where it came from—it remains a mystery to this day.

▶▶ At least 13 crystal skulls—found at various locations in Mexico, Central, and South America—were presented to museums and collectors during the 19th and early 20th centuries.

▶▶ Despite testing, nobody knows where the skulls come from. It is said that they are mysterious artifacts from ancient civilizations and that they possess spiritual powers.

▶▶ In 2005, a lucky Gentoo penguin narrowly escaped a pod of hungry killer whales off the coast of Antarctica when it jumped from the water into an inflatable boat full of tourists that happened to be floating nearby. The penguin then swam away but quickly returned to the boat to escape the lingering whales for a second time.

ANTARCTIC ANIMALS

credit: © BernardBreton/Fotolia.com

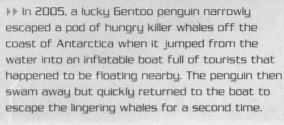

▶▶ Leopard seals are one of the most fearsome predators in the Antarctic, growing to over 10 feet long and weighing 1,000 pounds. They have been known to attack humans, but their main prey is penguins and other seals, which they catch in their powerful jaws.

▶▶ They are named leopard seals because of their sharp teeth and spotted skin.

▶▶ Killer whales are surprising hunters: they tip penguins off ice floes and will ride waves onto land to grab seals.

▶▶ Killer whales can swim at 19 miles an hour, weigh up to 10 tons and grow to 33 feet in length.

▶▶ Despite its fearsome name, there is no record of anyone being killed by a killer whale in the wild.

▶▶ ICE WATER SWIMMER

British adventurer Lewis Gordon-Pugh specializes in swimming in extremely cold water, and he has swum closer to the South Pole than anyone else.

▶▶ In 2005, Lewis swam for 1,100 yards through freezing water in the Antarctic. It took him 18 minutes and he wore only swimming shorts, a cap and goggles.

▶▶ He completed this swim on the anniversary of Roald Amundsen becoming the first man to reach the South Pole in 1911.

▶▶ Lewis relies on mental strength to complete his freezing swims, despite losing the feeling in his limbs in the water.

credit: Terje Eggum/Scanpix, Camera Press London

▶▶ In his lifetime, Ripley traveled over 450,000 miles looking for oddities—the distance from Earth to the Moon and back again.

▶▶ Ripley had a large collection of cars, but he couldn't drive. He also bought a Chinese sailing boat, called Mon Lei, but he couldn't swim.

▶▶ Ripley was so popular that his weekly mailbag often exceeded 170,000 letters, all full of weird and wacky suggestions for his cartoon strip.

▶▶ He kept a boa constrictor 20 feet long as a pet in his New York home.

In 1918, Robert Ripley became fascinated by strange facts while he was working as a cartoonist at the *New York Globe*. He was passionate about travel and, by 1940, had visited no fewer than 201 countries, gathering artifacts and searching for stories that would be right for his column, which he named Believe It or Not!

▶▶ Ripley's Believe It or Not! cartoon is the longest-running cartoon strip in the world, read in 42 countries and 17 languages every day.

Ripley bought an island estate at Mamaroneck, New York, and filled the huge house there with unusual objects and odd creatures that he'd collected on his explorations.

PACKED WITH FUN & GAMES, THE **RBI** WEBSITE IS HERE! CHECK IT OUT

REVIEWS

DOWNLOADS

MAPS & DATA

FUN!

MORE TEAM TALK

THE NEXT FILES